LUCKEY K.D.

love is dangerous

a dance through lifetimes

First edition

ISBN: 9798991031936

This book was professionally typeset on Reedsy.
Find out more at reedsy.com

Contents

Acknowledgement

Writing this book has been a journey of passion, persistence, and inspiration, and I would not have been able to complete it without the support of many incredible individuals. Thank you for embarking on this journey with Ren and Latisha. Your enthusiasm and support mean the world to me, and I hope this story resonates with you as deeply as it does with me.

With heartfelt thanks,

Luckey K.D.

THE SHAMAN

Nimble limbs. Blades of grass rustling. Heavy breathing. A yell. An arrow clicking off the bow and whizzing through the air. A stumble. A scream. A fall.

Silence!

Ren and Latisha huddled behind a fallen branch, hidden amidst shrubs and grasses. Darkness covered their lair like a blanket.

Ren made the sibilant sign of whispering with his hand across his thin lips. Latisha had been nursing the pain in her foot. She was forced to stay silent and possibly hold her breath.

"This way!" a man called in the distance.

Footsteps thumped closer, ruffling through the grasses. Ren and Latisha backed the pathway, not daring to look. They seemed confident their pursuers wouldn't look behind the branches.

Boots broke the silence as they stomped down the pathway. Ren and Latisha were as still as statues. The footsteps sounded as though they were directly underneath the path, with the layer of soil over their heads a few inches thick.

But without stopping, the men thumped past the branch, heading deeper into the forest. Ren stared vacantly while listening as the footsteps receded into the dark.

The forest regained quiescence, offering the nocturnals a chance for their voices to be heard.

Ren scrambled up on his knees as quietly as possible. His head slowly peeked over the branch. He scanned the area the same way a predator would do. But the men were nowhere in sight.

He got on his feet. "Latisha," he called in a whisper, putting out his hand behind him.

Latisha took his hand. Dry leaves shuffled around her as she got on her feet, too – a light wince etched up on her face. Her toes hurt a bit. But she would have to nurse it quietly until they had safely eluded the men.

They crept out of their lair. They must have wished their eyes were as keen as those of a cat's in the dark. But as rays of moonlight split through the crown, breaking the thick film of darkness at different points, all they could see were trees. Giant redwood and sequoia stood like columns in a fort, perhaps giving cover to their pursuers.

"This way."

Holding her hand the same way a mother would do her child, Ren led Latisha through a path in the opposite direction. Latisha was more careful this time. They still had a long way to go. A big injury wouldn't do them any good.

But as they skipped down the path, a voice called out:

"Here they are."

The men stormed out of their hiding places—about five, maybe more—and chased after Ren and Latisha. They sprinted.

Ren did not let go of Latisha's hand. He held tight to it as they navigated the bushes and trees. But Latisha thought she was better off with her hands-free. So while they ran, she carefully untangled her hand.

It was not a mistake, for she immediately turned on the jets. Her hands and legs flailed like windmills as she maneuvered the trees, leaping over fallen branches and thickets. She heard the click of an arrow off a crossbar. She looked back. As suspected, the arrow was coming right at her. She swerved to the right, and the arrow tore through the bark of a tree. But even as she maintained her balance, she had no idea another arrow was coming.

She zipped past a couple of trees and leaped over a hole. At this time, the arrow was a few centimeters away. The archer must have thought he finally got her. But a split-second thought made her look back. And with the reflex of a mongoose, she ducked. The arrow missed her head by a few inches. Perhaps it caught some strands of her hair on its way.

Ren himself had just escaped being hit by an arrow. He and Latisha kept a distance between them yet looked out for each other. He had gained some extra speed, too, as she unlocked her hand. And with ease, he broke through the film of darkness and rays of moonlight. His athletic frame and that of Latisha provided the agility of a Cheetah.

Their pursuers were relentless, however. Their boots stomped the ground like they were in a battleground. With their crossbows, they fired arrows again and again. But they hadn't quite nailed it yet.

Latisha gulped in mouthfuls of air as she ran. Trails of her breath could be seen in the air at areas illuminated by the moonlight. Her muscles were starting to experience fatigue, evident in her slower pace. But she had to keep moving. Ren noticed it, too. Gradually, he began to close the gap between them while looking for a safe spot for them to hide.

Latisha had just made it past a tree when a hand suddenly grabbed her and pulled her under its cover. A sharp scream echoed down the walls of the forest. Ren looked and changed course at once, charging toward the tree.

A man was behind the tree with Latisha. It didn't seem like he wanted to harm her. In fact, it looked more like he wanted to help them. He had his finger across his lips as he ushered Ren, who was a bit skeptical, to the cover of the tree.

The three of them hurdled behind the sequoia, with the man in front of the other two shielding them. They kept an eye out for their pursuers. Their chests rose and fell heavily as they swallowed mouthfuls of air, staring at this man in front of them with doubt on their faces.

The men stormed past the tree, not looking behind it. Even if they did, they might not have seen Latisha and the others, for it seemed like the darkness here was thicker than other places in the forest.

As their footsteps faded away, tranquility returned. The men looked back at Latisha and Ren. Their faces were a bit obscure in the dark, and the man wearing a hooded robe made it more difficult to make out his face.

"Come with me." He headed down a path perpendicular to that the men had gone.

But reluctance kept their feet on the spot. Ren wrapped his fingers around Latisha's wrists protectively. "We cannot come with you. We do not know who you are."

The man walked back to the tree and took off his hood. But in the dark, it was just the same as having it on. "My name is Claudius. I am a Shaman. I sensed your trouble in my abode, and the spirits led me here to help you."

Latisha thought he might have something to tell them about their quest. But she wanted to confirm again. "You are a Shaman?"

"Yes, I am. It is not safe out here. Join me in my abode, and I will show you a safe passage out of the forest."

He turned and continued on his way. Ren and Latisha looked at each other, communicating their thoughts. And breaking away from the reluctance tugging at their muscles, they followed Claudius.

Had Latisha and Ren not walked with Claudius, they would not have known a path lay between these grasses. It became more apparent as they walked. The men would have been combing other parts of the forest, looking for them, but it seemed like they were safe now.

Like a water trail, the path twisted and turned. Claudius did not say a word to his guests. He simply led them along, with the hood thrown back over his head. Ren clutched on Latisha's wrist. His eyes darted about as he sized up the surroundings suspiciously. If he made one wrong move, he would drag her along with him. All Latisha wanted was to talk with Claudius.

In the distance, a cabin nestled amidst a wall of conifers. A lantern hung down the roof outside, lighting the surroundings.

"That's my abode," Claudius revealed. It appeared he could sense their nervousness.

They glanced at each other and then settled their eyes at the cabin. Claudius led them on until they finally got to it.

Claudius unhooked the lantern from the roof and held it over his face. "Please come in."

The light had revealed a straight nose and small eyes. Just beneath his right eye was what Ren thought looked like a tattoo. Although it got him a little more nervous, he kept calm. He might get a chance to ask him about it later. Even so, reluctance acted on his legs as he followed Claudius through the door, with Latisha tagging along.

They sat on the floor, the lantern between them. The guests had scanned the room upon coming in. On the opposite walls were two medallions hanging from a nail. There were also some markings on the wall—one of which was a pentagon. A few totems lay here and there at the corners, leaving a wide space in the middle of the room. A door on the north wall led to other parts of the cabin.

Claudius had taken off the hood over his head. Now, his guests stared into his beady eyes as they talked.

"You mind telling me who you are and why you are in this forest at this time?" He glanced from one to the other.

It took Ren a moment to fight his hesitance to speak: "My name is Ren, and this is my lover, Latisha. We were passing through the forest."

"It is dangerous. The Marcas are always out there, hunting for their next victim."

Latisha's eyes flashed. "The Marcas? Who are they?"

Claudius adjusted his position. "Slave traders. And they would not have stopped until they got hold of you. If I may ask… where were you going?"

"We were looking for answers," Latisha blurted. She did not bother to look at Ren, for she knew he would have objected to revealing their movements to Claudius.

"Answers? Answers to what?" Claudius' eyes glinted with curiosity.

"To the Curse of Reincarnation," Ren answered.

"Oh," Claudius raised a brow, "I thought as much."

The lovers looked at each other briefly. "What do you mean," Ren asked.

"Your names: Ren and Latisha. Those were names given to the first lovers that were cursed to reincarnate for all eternity."

There was a spark in Latisha's eyes. It appeared Claudius had the answer to their problem.

"We are looking for whoever might have an idea on how we can break the curse," Ren told him.

Claudius took a deep breath, and his shoulders dropped. "I am not sure you will find such a person. It is a powerful curse. Only a deity can break it. And that, I doubt you will find."

The lovers did not say a word. Ren's Adam's apple bobbed up and down his throat.

"You mean there is nothing we can do about it?" intoned Latisha, disbelief in her voice. "This is our 7th reincarnation through generations…"

"But is reincarnation not meant to be a blessing? I mean, you have the chance to complete whatever you were not able to complete in your previous life."

"That, perhaps, would be the case if one came in a different body, as a different entity," Ren cut in. "We have looked the same through generations…"

"Makes it all better…"

"No, it does not," Latisha snapped. "We wish to put these bodies to rest."

Claudius was quiet this time. Latisha looked at the orange flame swaying gently in the lantern. If only it could give her the answers she wanted. She was starting to lose hope of Claudius helping them.

"I think I have an idea someone that might have the answers you seek." Claudius broke the brief moment of silence.

Latisha looked up from the lantern – her eyes had suddenly picked up some curiosity in them. "Who?"

"I do not know his name, but you will find him in the Island of Reprieve."

Ren cocked a brow. "That is quite far from here."

"It is. But I believe he will have answers to your questions. He is a descendant of the Old Religion."

"Thank you. We have to go now."

"I suggest you pass the night here. It is dangerous out there…"

With the Marcas possibly still scouting the forest for them, the lovers had no choice. But it wasn't a fruitless journey, after all. Now they had a destination. Now, they were convinced there was someone out there who could help them.

THE ABDUCTION

Ren and Latisha sat by the fire. They had left Claudius' abode less than an hour ago. He had shown them a safe passageway. Along the way, Latisha had requested that they rest a while.

She gazed into the fire as it crackled like burning trees, sending tiny sparks into the air. "How long do you think it will take us to get to the Island of Reprieve?"

Ren rubbed his hands together and brought them near the flame. "A day. That is if we do not encounter any trouble on our way."

She looked up at him. "You did not think Claudius could help us."

"No. Shamans have great knowledge about curses, but not one as deep as this."

Latisha exhaled deeply. The air from her nostrils made the flame before her sway. "I wish that man at Island of Reprieve would have all the answers we need. I am tired of looking."

"Like Claudius said, he is a descendant of the Old Religion. I believe he will have all the answers we need."

Latisha nodded and looked around. Hey, eyes met the trees standing like pillars across the forest. The thick film of the night was fast fading away. Birds that announced the presence of dawn were arriving for the great assembly.

"Honestly, I do not want us to die off in this generation without breaking the curse." Latisha's voice had taken the tone of misery.

"I believe we won't…"

"I hope so. I am sated with coming back to life and taking on the same quest. The 7th time!"

Ren could feel the depression in her words. Her voice seemed hopeless. The leaves rustled as he got on his feet. He moved over to her and sat beside her, draping his arm across her shoulders.

"Even if we would return, it would be in different bodies, almost different personalities, and of course, different goals."

Latisha looked at him, doubt gleaming in her blue downturned eyes. "These were almost the same words you told me in our previous lifetime."

Ren reassured in a soft, convincing tone of voice. "They will come to pass this time."

Latisha's eyes fell on his lips. In the orange flame, they looked more appealing than ever. Ren gazed rather into her eyes, perhaps admiring the image of the sparks from the fire.

"I just want us to get old together and die," she lamented. "There are too many troubles in the world to witness them the 8th time."

Ren placed his index across her lips. "That is not going to happen."

He kissed her lips softly – the same lips he had kissed through 7 lifetimes. They tasted and felt just like the very first day. She loved it, and then she kissed him back. Their lips smacked as the fire crackled, sending sparks into the air like fireworks. Ren slid his hand up her breasts and fondled them like they were going to fall off if he went too hard. Latisha ground her body against his, kissing him with greater passion.

However, this moment lasted for a short time. Latisha heard it first and pulled out.

"Can you hear that?" Tension hung in her eyes.

"I cannot hear anything. What is it?" intoned Ren.

"Footsteps! They are coming this way." She scrambled up on her feet, raining bits of dried leaves and sand.

Ren got on his feet, too. As he was about to put out the fire, he realized they were surrounded. It was dawn at this time, and the forest could boast of some degree of brightness.

Ren quickly moved to where Latisha was, grabbing a smoldering stick from the fire. Latisha had a stick in her hand, too.

"Who are you?" Ren asked, glancing across the 7 faces that had surrounded them.

The men—all of them — were putting on brown pants and red jackets, which looked like some kind of uniform. Some had crossbows, others had clubs, and others had swords.

"Found you!" one of them spoke in a mildly casual tone.

Ren clutched at the stick in his hand while appearing to cover Latisha. "What do you mean?"

Another man stepped forward. With the color of his shirt a bit darker than those of the others, he appeared to be their leader. "We are agents of a group of people known as *Apokata*. Our queen wants you. You do not have a choice but to come with us quietly."

"We are not going anywhere…"

"Not 'we', but 'you'. We want you to come with us."

"And why will I do that and abandon my own cause?"

The man looked at the others and then back at Ren. "We do not intend to apply force, but we will if you remain adamant."

"Look, I do not care who you are. But I am not going anywhere with you."

Ren took his lover by the hand and tried to walk away. But one of the men stood in their way, looking a bit swollen as a way of intimidation.

"Like I said, we would apply force if necessary. Do not worry – I am sure your woman will do just fine without you."

If Ren was ever going to consider their request, he would change his mind at this statement. He and Latisha couldn't do without each other. He fixed the man an angry stare, but it was for a moment.

"Leave my way!" he warned, raising the smoldering stick in his hand.

The agent looked deep into his eyes, hitting the club on his hand threateningly. "You will have to do more than that."

Latisha stormed in front of Ren. "Well, tell your queen that he does not want her. Now leave our way, or you will regret it."

The agent looked at the others, and they all chuckled. But Latisha wouldn't take that disrespect. She stormed forward and tried to shove the man out of the way. He grabbed her instead. Ren wanted to clobber the agent's head with the stick, but another agent quickly pulled him backward, grabbed his hands, and shook it off. Two others stormed in and grabbed him.

"LET ME GO," Latisha yelled as she kicked and bucked.

The anxiety in her voice fuelled Ren's effort to fight free. Veins popped out of his neck – those across his forehead threatened to break through the thin skin on his forehead. But his strength was no match for those of the men. Four of them had him in their grip.

"Bring him along, and you two can take care of her the way you deem fit."

The leader led the way as the other four agents dragged Ren along. He charged at them with all his might. His biceps bulged as he tried to break free from the man's grip. He might have fought free if it was only one of them and not four.

Latisha was probably more stubborn than the agents could handle. With Ren being dragged farther and farther away from her, adrenaline pumped through her muscles. The agents clung on with their last bit of strength.

Gradually, Ren and the others dissolved into the thick cloud of dew and out of sight. Latisha did not stop calling his name all the while.

"Now what shall we do with… you?" one of the agents asked.

His colleague laughed and looked behind Latisha. "She looks appetizing."

"You know what I am talking about, brother. The queen can have him while we have her."

They both broke off with laughter.

"Not even in your dreams," Latisha spat.

She almost slipped out of their hands. But the second man managed to gain a tighter grip at once, nearly crushing her right bicep. Her cheeks had turned crimson. The men looked at each other.

"Come here."

They dragged her behind a nearby tree.

"REN! SOMEBODY HELP!" she screamed.

But the men seemed certain that no one would hear her, for they laughed even louder as they forced her to a supine position. She flung her legs like a cockroach that had fallen on its back, refusing to be subdued. Droplets of sweat had spread on the men's forehead. They may have the upper hand, but they would admit that this apparently lowly girl was giving them a hard time.

They finally managed to subdue her. Even so, she did not stop fighting. She seemed to have springs in her legs that wouldn't stop contracting and relaxing.

One man pinned her arms to the ground. The other tried to take her pants off. Somehow, she found her fingers digging through the soil. And wasting no time, she packed a handful of sand and threw it at the man, keeping her upper body on the ground. She wasn't sure she would hit the target. But she actually did.

The man yelled, with his eyes shut. He let go of Latisha's right hand to rub his own eyes. Big mistake!

She parked more of the sand and spattered it directly on his face this time. Some of it could have gone into his eyes, for he let go of the other hand, too. At the same time, Latisha flung her leg. It caught the other agent on the jaw, throwing his head backward. Latisha scrambled up on her feet.

She reached for the club lying next to her and smashed the agent's head. He dropped to the ground and did not move again. She charged at the other agent, who was still groping about and rubbing his eyes. The club swung in the air like a gladiator's sword and crashed on his head. He, too, fell to the ground and remained motionless.

Latisha dropped the club and looked around frantically. Daylight had lightened up the forest. Trees towered high like pillars in the Babylonian era. Birds flapped from one treetop to another, rustling the leaves and chirping. And with the sun peeking out of the horizon, it was starting to thaw.

She shot off at once down the road the other agents had gone down. She hoped they hadn't gone too far. It was a risky attempt, but even riskier was continuing the journey without Ren.

RESCUE FROM THE APOKATA

Latisha had no idea where she was going. For starters, she didn't even know who these Apokata were. She hadn't heard about them before. Now, she had to look for their settlement for the sake of her partner. She made her way through the forest. There was no path laid out except the one she carved for herself. She believed the Apokata wouldn't settle in the forest, and so she had to find her way out.

But having walked all day, it seemed like she was never going to reach the edge of the forest. At this point, her eyes were droopy. A mist of sweat trailed her forehead. She needed somewhere to calm her breath. And having found a safe spot at the foot of a willow tree, she settled in.

She threw her head back against the tree, taking in mouthfuls of air. The dryness in her throat had her swallowing every drop of saliva in her mouth. The dry air was evidence that there was no source of water nearby. She would have to make do with the shade and the refreshing breeze the tree provided.

It was so comfortable here. Sleep was starting to creep into her eyes. But not in a place like this. Danger lurked behind the trees, everywhere.

She raised her head and shook it. But the sleep did not fall off. It returned the moment she leaned her head on the tree again.

"Not safe sleeping in a forest like this," a voice spoke.

It got Latisha jumping like a startled rabbit. Impulsively, she reached for the stick next to her, without looking at the man who had spoken. She grabbed the stick and then looked up.

He was putting on what looked like a military coat. The red color left the big white buttons in sharp contrast. He had his golden hair in a French plait. With his arms folded behind and shifty eyes, Latisha thought he looked like a magician of some sort.

He did not as much as flinching a muscle when she clambered up and went for the stick. He merely batted his thick lashes. The adrenaline rush in Latisha drained off her pipes at the sight of this strange yet funny-looking man.

Eyes wild, she glared at him. "Who are you?"

"You are Latisha Longman, betrothed by a reincarnation curse to Ren Huckleberry."

Latisha went pale in the face. She looked around as if searching for the spirit speaking through this man.

"I ask again: who are you?" She tightened up her countenance.

"I am Fred De Seer, and I can tell that you're on a journey to the Island of the Reprieve with your partner who, as we speak, is being cleaned up for the mating ritual with the queen of Apokata."

Latisha barely looked away from him. She took two steps closer, with the stick still in her hand. "What do you know about the reincarnation curse?"

Fred smiled. But it vanished as quickly as it came. "Not much. All I do know is that time is not on your side."

Latisha stared hard at him, not saying a word. And then she took another step closer. "Why do I feel like you know more about this curse?"

"My apologies, but I have only said what I am allowed to say."

"And what do you mean by 'time is not on your side'? Are we missing something?"

"You will find out soon enough. For now, you have to hurry and rescue your partner."

Latisha realized it was pointless to press further. No matter how hard she tried to make him say more, he wasn't going to say more.

"The Apokata: you know where I can find them?" she inquired.

"They live in the Palm Field, not far from the White River."

"And…"

"In the east."

Latisha swallowed back the rest of the words. Her countenance had lightened. "Thank you."

She threw away the stick in her hand. Dry leaves and twigs crunched underfoot as she trudged away.

"East!" Fred reminded her. She looked. "It is this way." He pointed.

"Oh…" She nodded and walked behind him.

"One more thing, Latisha: you will realize that the curse is a result of a debt. And this curse would not have existed if someone had not initiated it."

After he had said these, he walked away, leaving Latisha in even greater confusion. She was still trying to grasp what he meant by time not being on their side, and now she had to deal with the knowledge that someone initiated the curse. How was that even possible?

She stood at the spot even after Fred had gone out of sight, wondering who it could be. But being reminded that Ren was going through some cleansing for the mating ritual, she bolted off.

The direction Fred had pointed led Latisha to the edge of the forest. She had only made brief stops to catch her breath along the way. And now, as she made it out to the pathway beyond the forest's edge, she could see the Palm Field about a hundred meters away. The White River was twice that distance on the right.

Latisha crossed the pathway toward Palm Field. In her mind, a conversation was going on about how to rescue Ren. She couldn't just barge in and demand that he be freed; her movements had to be discreet.

It was a rural settlement, with small houses scattered out in every direction. About three palm trees surrounded every house, forming a wall. White and green were the distinctive colors here—from clothes to housing. The people went about in the spirit of a new day, oblivious to the stalker behind the tree.

Latisha observed their activities. She saw two men dressed like the ones that attacked her and Ren. She surmised they could be the queen's guards. Her eyes walked with them through the deeper ends of the Field – and then they disappeared behind a building. The queen's quarters could be around there, she thought.

Her eyes made a map through the settlement, from one tree to another. She would have to be careful so as not to be seen by any of the men who took Ren.

And now, she meandered from tree to tree, going deeper into the settlement. Although she moved through the edges, some of the people spotted her. But she was not perceived as a threat. Perhaps it was due to the way she moved casually from one tree to another, yet keeping a close eye on the guards.

While she strolled to the next tree, she saw the two guards she had defeated in the forest. They were rubbing their heads and walking down the path the first two guards walked. It was confirmed where the queen's quarter was.

She followed the men, taking cover behind trees whenever they turned their heads. The mist from the river some distance away filled her lungs and fueled her muscles as she crept forward.

At what looked like the center of the settlement, a house stood. It was built like a ranch house, bigger than every other house in the settlement. Palm fronds bordered the narrow walkways extending from both sides of the house, which led to thatched cottages. Guards hung around, some of them carrying crossbows. Latisha observed carefully as they moved from one part of the house to another.

The royal quarters were at the center of Palm Field, making it difficult to observe them from behind. The gate was open, and she would be caught. A rescue mission would have been better done in the cover of darkness, but she feared it would have been too late by then.

She leaned against the tree and threw her face skyward. It was a clear white-and-blue morning. The palm branches swayed in the breeze, raining down some refreshments. She inhaled deeply and closed her eyes.

But as if touched by some force, she looked at the quarters again. Ren was being led by two guards from the cottage toward the main building. He only had his underwear on, bound at the wrists with a chain like a slave.

Regardless of the number of guards out here, Latisha thought this was the perfect time to launch a rescue attempt. She looked up at the sky once again, hooding her eyes with her hand and squinting. The sun was almost reaching the middle of the sky. There was a possibility the mating ritual would begin when it did. It would be over for her if Ren went into the quarters. Rescuing him was now or never.

She looked around the tree and found a stone the size of the fist of an adult male. Next to it was a wood as big as the handle of an axe. She padded closer and picked them up. She hated that Ren wasn't looking up. She would have put herself in his view. Perhaps he did not think she would try to rescue him.

She lobbed the stone in the men's direction, hoping Ren would take advantage of the distraction. It landed on a guard's head. He yelled and fell to the ground, bleeding from the spot. The men stood on high alert. With their crossbows positioned for a counterattack, their searching eyes combed the surroundings. Those leading Ren quickly headed for cover behind the raft.

But Ren understood the message. The first guard went behind the raft. The other guard pushed him through. As he stumbled in, he rammed his weight against the first guard. The other man charged in, but he got a jaw-breaking kick to the face. Ren quickly got on his feet and made for the exit.

Latisha had spotted the commotion even before it started. Now she ran behind a tree. She wanted the men to see her. It was a way to divert some of their attention from Ren. And it worked.

"There she is!" a guard yelled.

About seven of them went after her – four others went after Ren in the opposite direction. Through the path he had taken, the White River would have been his best option for an escape. But he was not a good swimmer.

The men fired shot after shot – some of them narrowly missing the target. Ren sprinted through the trees and bushes, ducking and taking cover behind the trees.

The whole community went agog as Latisha made her through Palm Field. Everyone scampered for safety as the men fired arrows in different directions. Stray arrows hit some of the people – maybe two or three casualties lay on the ground. The rest of the arrows tore through the trees and houses.

Latisha crossed the path that separated the plains from the forest. And just as she stumbled into the forest, she heard her name echo across the walls. Ren! Yes, talk about speed: those guards were no match for him. Latisha always made jokes of him being a descendant of the Impala family. Most times, she had to hold his hand to keep up. So it wasn't surprising to her how he managed to make it to the forest before she even did.

As she turned in the direction of his voice, an arrow zipped past her face, slicing through her ear. She placed her hand on it and continued to run. It was probably a small cut.

"REN!" she called.

"LATISHA!" he answered.

That was to decipher which way to follow after that interruption. At the same time, it could betray them to their pursuers. They simply hoped to find each other before then.

With fatigue building up in her muscles, Latisha wasn't sure how far she could go. Her mouth gaped as she gulped down fuel for her muscles. She looked back. Although the men were nowhere in sight, she feared they could be somewhere close. But when she turned, she saw him about five trees away.

Ren was standing by a tree, looking around. It was probably how far her voice had led him.

"Ren!"

He looked and then ran toward her. And when they met, she wrapped her arms around him. He would have done the same, but he still had his hand in a chain. Latisha withdrew and dropped a kiss on his lips. He looked like he wanted more, but there was no time for something passionate.

"Come on," she chivvied him as though she had prepared somewhere safe for them.

The men must have lost their way, for even as the partners took off again, there was no sign of them anywhere.

ISLAND OF REPRIEVE

On their way through the forest, Ren had found an axe at the foot of a stump. It was so rusty it appeared to have been there for decades. But it was the only weapon they had found for the chain.

Ren had set his wrists on the stump. And with the axe, Latisha had broken the chain in one powerful hit. Ren had once again felt the significance of freedom.

They had spent the whole day looking for a safe spot in the forest. Along the way, they had found a shirt and trousers buried amidst a heap of human bones – something to cover Ren's nakedness.

Latisha stood by the small stream flowing through the forest. The trousers and shirt were spread out on the branches of a small ash tree. "You have not said anything about the ritual, Ren."

"Maybe it is because there is nothing special about it." Ren put the wood together and then began to pick some dried leaves.

Latisha walked toward him. "I don't understand."

"They simply took off my clothes, bathed me with colored water, and then applied some sweet-smelling oil all over my body."

"And you say there is nothing special about it? What more were you expecting them to do?" Latisha stood next to him as he arranged the leaves over the woods.

"Perhaps some kind of magic…"

Latisha smirked. "Do you not think the magic would have incapacitated you?"

Ren struck the chain against the ax, creating a spark that ignited the leaves. Wisps of smoke wriggled up in the air.

"I only thought they would use magic, not like I wanted them to."

Latisha glanced from the bulk of his chest and the ridges on his abdomen down his groin area. "That bath:" she moved closer, wetting her upper lip "Are you sure it was all they did to you?"

Ren slid his hand around her waist and pulled her closer. "Not at all." He spoke in a voice that aroused her senses. "They also ignited a fire in me that only you, my darling, can put out."

He kissed her lips, sliding his left hand behind her neck while the right kept her in position. She kissed him with the same passion, hands gliding up his body ridges. Ren slid up her breasts and began to caress them softly, from whence his fingers found the buttons.

As he exposed a pair of tear-drop-shaped breasts, she caught his underwear. They both had their lips locked on all the while. Latisha gently massaged his loins, giving more weight to his manliness. She herself let out a gasp as he kissed from her neck down her chest. His tongue smacked upon reaching her breasts. And with the softness of his lips and tongue, he worshipped on her sanctuary. Latisha moaned softly, breathing through her mouth. It was not because she was being chased this time, but being on the peak of ecstasy.

Ren gently put her down on the ground, kissing and nibbling on every bit of flesh. And right there, by the fire, they strengthened their bond and reveled in their sacredness.

* * *

"That, over there, is the Island of Reprieve," Latisha pointed.

It was less than a hundred meters away, in the middle of a river that appeared green on the surface. A canoe was by the riverbank as if waiting for them.

Their shoes were almost worn out from walking all day. When they arrived by the river, they wasted no time drinking from it and washing their faces.

"Why does it have to be so far into the water?" Ren lamented, brushing off drops of water from his beard.

Latisha looked at him like he had just said the stupidest thing she had ever heard. She walked to the canoe and tried to pull it ashore. "Help me," she requested.

Ren sighed and joined her.

After they had dragged a quarter of the canoe ashore, Latisha got on it. Ren grabbed the paddle.

He gathered some momentum and pushed the canoe back into the water. As soon as it touched the water, he hopped on it and stirred it toward the island with the paddle.

They were not certain of what or whom they would find on the island. They did not even know the name of the man they were looking for. But they hoped that when they did find him, he would be willing to help. Hitherto, Latisha had told Ren what Fred De Seer had revealed. He had asked the same question: 'Who could have initiated the curse?'

As they glided closer, the island began to reveal itself. Conifers formed a wall at the edges. Somewhere in the middle of the island was a structure made of rocks. It looked more like a temple. The man they were looking for definitely resided within its walls, Latisha thought.

"It does not look like anyone lives there," Ren observed as they disembarked from the canoe.

"You would not know until we go inside," Latisha replied.

Together, they pulled the canoe ashore and headed toward the structure. Latisha had merely glanced skyward when she noticed something strange.

"Ren, look up."

A flock of vultures encircled the temple, the same way they would do over a dying animal.

"That's not a good sign," Ren commented. "We should hurry."

He took the lead, and Latisha followed. They kept glancing skyward, hoping the vultures would disperse. Instead, more of them joined the parade.

The temple stood several meters off the ground, entirely made of boulders.

Thinking about how they got up to that height would hurt. Between the walls was a narrow entrance—so narrow that Latisha and Ren had to go through it, turning sideways.

The inside of the table was circular. Surrounded by walls, it seemed like it was in a well. At the center was a round table carved out of stones. Beyond this table was an elevated portion of the temple. Rocks lay here and there. A boulder nearly the size of a canoe occupied the space in this area. It was shaped like a tray. A man sprawled on it like it was a mattress.

"What happened to him?" Latisha asked, pointing.

"We would have to get closer to find out," Ren answered.

The vultures overhead were gathering in their numbers, expectant of a good feast. Ren proceeded to the man while Latisha kept watch. She looked from one end of the wall to another. The stones glistened with water as the evening sun reflected on them.

His hair was as white and soft as wool. Ren preferred to believe he was alive, even though he doubted it.

"Hello."

The man's hair and beard swayed lightly in the wind, perhaps redirecting the sound of Ren's voice.

He stretched his neck to get a better look at the man's face. He could be meditating or something. "Hello, sir. Can you hear me?"

Latisha leveled up the distance between her and Ren. "I doubt he can hear you. You should go closer."

That was probably not the advice Ren was looking for, but it was inevitable. He was not scared; he just did not want to overstep his boundaries.

He moved closer and hesitantly took the man's hand hanging down the rock. As he wrapped his fingers around the wrist, he looked at Latisha. "It's cold."

"What?"

She moved in and climbed up the rock, nervous in her bones. Then she took the other hand. It felt cold, too. She went on her knees and pressed her ear against the man's chest.

After a minute, she raised her head, eyes wild as she gazed at Ren. "He is dead."

"I thought so, too."

She looked down at the body again. Suddenly realizing what his death could mean, she tapped his hand.

"Wake up! Wake up!" She pushed and pulled on the body. "You cannot die. Please wake up!"

It was the man they had come to see – the only man who might have answers to their questions like Claudius had said. His long, green robe and the red medallion hanging down his neck showed he was probably a priest. A priest of the old religion would have indeed had the answers to their questions. Now, he lived no more.

Latisha tugged at his robe, refusing to accept that he was dead. "Please wake up! You cannot die. Not now, please!"

Ren had also realized the enormity of his death. He stood by the rock with an unsteady gaze at the body. His heart weighed on his chest. They had been so close, so close at finding answers to their questions. They would have to start all over again.

The man's body swayed back and forth as Latisha continued to pull on it, crying for him to wake up. With those eyes shimmering like glass, perhaps he would have woken up if he could hear her.

Ren took her by the hand. "It's okay. We have to go."

He helped her down the rock and hugged her. She sobbed gently on his shoulder as she rubbed down on her hair, gazing at the body behind her and wishing it could move.

"We must not give up, darling. I think I have an idea of what we should do next."

Latisha sniffed back the rest of her tears and withdrew from his shoulder. Her eyes were a bit swollen - and when she blinked, a teardrop fell off her eyes and rolled down her cheek.

"The medallion on his chest carries a symbol. With it, we could find someone else who might have an idea on how to break the curse."

Latisha looked back at the medallion, Ren's hands sliding down her shoulders. It had a crescent moon in the shape of a 'C' and a star hanging between the curves. Above the crescent was what looked like a cross, with the upper bar curved like a horseshoe and joining the central point.

She turned back at Ren. "Do you think we should take it off him? There could be consequences."

Ren rubbed on her hair. "That is the only way to convince someone of what we are looking for."

"Yet the consequences are grave."

Latisha grabbed Ren's hand in shock as they shot a look at the direction the voice had come.

A woman stood by the rock at the center of the temple. She was dressed in a green robe, like the dead man. Hanging down her neck was a medallion that looked just the same as that on the man. She held a staff that had a ball the size of an orange on it. This ball glittered like it had a galaxy of stars in it.

Ren looked around as if trying to figure out how she managed to gain entrance into the temple. "Who are you?"

"I am Dara, high priestess of the old religion. The man lying behind you was the supreme priest of the old religion. Just like me, he was a devoted servant."

Latisha looked at the man once again as if to confirm what the priestess had said. "A supreme priest dies like a commoner?" She turned back, brows furrowed.

"It may seem that way to you, but to a priest, it is the greatest honor." She moved her head slightly to the right, sizing them up. "What are you doing here?"

"We seek knowledge…"

"Knowledge of the Curse of Reincarnation. I know."

Ren glanced at his partner. And with careful steps, they walked closer to the priestess. Latisha could hardly take her eyes off her golden hair and the gold bracelet around her wrist. She thought they glorified her so well.

"Please tell us: how do we break the curse?" Ren asked.

"Perhaps if you knew why the curse was pronounced upon you and how it was initiated, you would know how to break it."

"We do not know. Please tell us." Curiosity burned in the lovers' eyes. It was a moment they wished they could invade the priestess' memory bank.

Priestess Dara walked past them. Their eyes followed her to the rock the priest lay.

"In your first lifetime, you found a sword buried in the rocks in the Woods of Balanon. Do you remember?"

Inadmissible lines grew between Ren's brows. He looked at Latisha, who shook her head. "We cannot recall the event you speak about." He looked up at Priestess Dara.

"You ignorantly took the sword out of the Woods of Balanon and threw it into the River Uta…" Priestess Dara's voice faded off with the wind. It was perhaps to give the lovers some time to think.

Latisha's brain gyrated inside her as she tried to remember—Ren bullied him to come up with something. Returning as the same person made it possible for them to remember events in their past lives, but this particular event seemed to have eluded their memory.

"What you speak of happened in our first lifetime," Latisha spoke. "This is our 7th. Forgive us if we do not remember."

"The sword carries the symbol of the old religion. It binds the spirits of the 7 lords that govern the affairs of life since the beginning of time. The sword is meant to be in the Mighty Rocks, not in the depths of the River Uta. You brought the Reincarnation Curse upon yourselves when you threw the sword into the river. The spirits of the 7 lords want you to find the sword and take it back to the Mighty Rocks."

Ren swallowed hard, eyelids fluttering. He could feel Latisha's hands tightening around his forearm. She, too, could feel the tension brought on by Priestess Dara's words.

"Is that all we have to do to break the curse?" he inquired.

"When you find the sword, you must first take it to the 7 elders of the Apokata…"

"The what?" Latisha interrupted – her lips quirked up.

"Yes. They have been bestowed with cleansing powers. They will tell you what to do."

The lovers glanced at each other. That would be one difficult task.

"Thank you…" Ren concluded, but Latisha quickly interrupted him.

"No, wait!" She turned to Priestess Dara. "It seems you forgot to tell us how the curse was initiated."

The corner of Priestess Dara's lips went up in a smile. "I did not forget. I knew you would ask. Three days after you threw the sword into the river, your mother stood by the riverbank and prayed that you survive the plague – even if you don't, that you be granted easy passage to the other world. She cut herself and let the blood drop into the river. The drops traveled through the water and latched onto the sword. And so the curse was activated."

"My mother?" Ren's brows knitted. "But she never told me anything about it."

"You survived the plague, yes, but her blood activated the curse. And now it is a Karmic debt you must pay."

Latisha glanced at Ren as if reprimanding him for what his mother did.

Ren rubbed gently on her hand. "We have to go now."

"You were given 7 lifetimes to find the sword and return it to the Mighty Rocks. This is your final chance. You must break the curse and return the sword before the full moon of the lunisolar month. If you fail, your souls will be condemned to the dark pit for all eternity after you die."

Latisha's eyes flashed. "Following the solstice, that's barely 3 days away."

"Then you must hurry."

"All right. Thank you."

Latisha was still holding on to Ren as they made their way toward the exit. A few feet away from the passageway, Ren looked back. Priestess Dara was still looking at them.

"What about him?" He pointed at the body lying on the rock.

"You should worry about yourselves." He nodded and continued his way.

CAVE OF SKULLS

"Why can't we remember the beginning of our problems?" Ren questioned as they trudged along the windy road.

Latisha sighed. "We were always out in the woods when we first met. It must have happened during one of those times. The problem is: how do we convince the elders of Apokata to help us?"

"They would probably shoot us down on sight." Ren giggled.

"It's not funny. We have to get to the River Uta, find the sword, go to the Palm Field, and convince the elders to help us. And if they agree and the curse is broken, we must return the sword to the Mighty Rocks – all these in just 3 days."

Ren pouted his lips and let off some air between them. He was reminded of the consequences should they fail to keep to the time.

"I do not know the best way to convince the elders of Apokata to help us, but it can only be them, according to the Priestess."

"And what if they refuse? They lost some of their people while chasing after us."

Ren thought about that for a moment. "I think it's an obligation they must obey."

Latisha looked down the road. It reminded her of how far they had to go. "We must hurry…"

It was not a straight road to the River Uta. They followed the windy path through the woods. There was barely time to rest. They had only spared a few moments harvesting figs and berries. After they had had their fill, they went on their way.

The path through the woods led them to a creek. The arid grounds were covered with lilies and chrysanthemums, among other flowers. A monkey screeched and swung from one tree to another at the sight of them. They both looked up and hooded their eyes as droplets of water from the leaves rained on them.

"We got monkeys in here," Ren reported.

Latisha wiped some water drops off her forehead. "Of course, it's a rich source of food and water."

The leaves overhead rustled one more time. It was simply the monkey announcing their presence.

Somewhere in the creek was what looked like the ruins of a castle nestled amidst conifers and redwoods. A stream of water followed a channel that seemed to create a pathway through the creek. The water sloshed around their feet as Latisha and Ren traveled through it.

Latisha moved a twig out of her way. The droplets of water on it sprinkled on her face. She blew off the drop hanging on her lower lip. "So had your mother not let her blood drop into the river the curse would not have been activated. Do you think the 7 lords knew she would be at the river?"

Ren had his eyes on the ruins, but they returned to the water on the ground upon hearing Latisha's voice. "Since the curse needed drops of blood to be activated, yes, they knew she would be there. My question is: what if it was not my mother?"

"You mean the priestess could be lying?"

His brows snapped shut. "What? No, not at all. I mean: would the curse have been activated if it was the blood of a non-relative?"

"I don't think it would have…"

The water track guided them through the creek. A cave stood up ahead. They chatted on as they made their way toward it.

Ren climbed on a piece of rock on his way and dipped his feet back into the water. "You know: it may be arduous, but I am glad we finally found a way to break the curse."

"I feel so too, although I cannot quite get Claudius' voice off my head."

Ren looked at her briefly as if to be sure she hadn't been hypnotized. "How do you mean?"

"I feel instead of seeing it as a curse, we should be thankful."

"Thankful, you say?" Ren's eyes lit up. He couldn't help but be amazed at her words.

"Should we not be grateful that we reincarnate in our original forms? It gives us a chance to accomplish what we could not in our previous lifetime. It gives us the chance to love each other through generations and correct the mistakes we made. It also gives us the opportunity to witness the world's civilization as it grows. I feel it is more of a blessing than a curse, really."

There was sense in what she said, and Ren knew it. It was probably the reason he was quiet for a moment before realizing it. "You may be right, but like the priestess said, this is our last chance at lifting the curse. It was not meant to last forever. Besides, how much longer must we suffer these bones of ours?"

Reincarnation sounded better to Latisha than resting for all eternity. Perhaps if she could, she would make the curse last forever. However, that was a thought she wouldn't share with Ren. It would leave him more surprised and confused.

The stream wriggled its way into the cave, and it could be heard from the outside as it gurgled through. Latisha and Ren walked through the entrance. The lower temperature here left them with goosebumps spreading on their skin like leaf galls. The walls looked like they had just been washed, and the mosses and ferns grew on them like some kind of decoration.

"It seems there is no other way out of here," Latisha's voice echoed across the walls.

But Ren did not reply. His interest was in the writings on the wall. He gazed at them as they proceeded farther into the cave. "What language is this?"

Latisha went closer and looked. "I do not know about this, but these are hieroglyphs…"

"I know hieroglyphs, although I cannot read them. But this right here is far from my knowledge."

Latisha had already backed away from the wall. They still had a long way to go, and it seemed Ren had forgotten. "Come on," she chivied him.

They steered down the watercourse, looking from one end of the cave to another. Birds chirped and flapped in and out of the cave. Their echoes resounded across the walls. Some parts of the roof had stalactites growing from them. And the deeper they went, the colder it became.

The watercourse ended as it diverted and flowed through a crack in the wall. At this point, the lovers were standing before three pathways that looked more like tunnels. The pathway on the right was a long, narrow way. It was so dark they would need a torch to go through it. It was the same for the pathway on the left. But that right in front of them was grey. It seemed to have a source of light somewhere inside.

Latisha tipped herself sideways as though she could see the end of the tunnel in the middle. Her eyes darted between Ren and the pathway. She was apprehensive about going through it, and she made it clear. "What if we find another way? It could be dangerous there."

"Look around you, Latisha, does it look like there's another way out?" Ren questioned.

She did look around. The only way was through which they had come.

"We should not have come through this cave. We should have taken another way."

Ren knew where all that was coming from, so he did not bother to reply. He, too, was not certain where the pathway would lead them. But for how far they had come, it was worth a try.

"Come on." He led the way.

Latisha hung back for a moment, looking at Ren as he marched into the pathway. Her legs felt like they were at zero degrees.

Ren stopped just by the entrance, having noticed she wasn't coming along. "Is there a problem?" he inquired.

Latisha flicked a glance at him and at the path. She did not answer him.

Eventually, she summoned the courage to take a step toward it. Ren waited for her to get closer. He could see the anxiety in her blue eyes.

He took her hand as they plodded through the tunnel's thin gray light. The light source gradually became dimmer as they went, making it a bit difficult for Latisha to see.

She placed her hand on the wall as a guide and support. But then it felt rough, like rocks had been glued to its surface.

"The wall," she commented.

Ren placed his hand on it. "Yes, probably stones."

It had Latisha a bit more on the edge. She tightened her grip on Ren, hoping they would get out of this tunnel as quickly as possible.

It was starting to turn gray again, and Latisha noticed the skulls on the wall first.

"My goodness!" she cringed, wrapping her arms at Ren.

He held her in his protection. "It's okay. We are in the Cave of Skulls. They are harmless."

Latisha let out a breath of relief and loosened her grip on Ren. She knew they were harmless; she was just startled upon seeing them suddenly.

The skulls were intricately arranged on the walls in about ten rows from top to bottom. They stretched further and further as the lovers plodded through the tunnel. Latisha could hardly take her eyes off the sockets. They felt like a thousand and one reproachful eyes watching her, cursing and casting her out of their presence.

Ren led her on as they navigated the windy tunnel. It got brighter as they approached its end, narrower as the skulls became more densely packed. They could see the beam of the evening sun refracted on the wall. Limbs lighter and propelled by curiosity, they skipped faster.

And now, they emerged from the tunnel's windy shape into the light. It guided them on as they made it toward its source. Latisha couldn't wait to get out, and neither could the skulls.

The source of light was the sun. It turned out they made the right choice by going through the middle tunnel. It had led them out of the cave. The sun bathed them in its light straight from the blue sky, not obstructed by trees. For Latisha, it was refreshing to see the sun again, to see the earth's biodiversity.

Ren had something else bothering him, however. Less than 20 meters away was a range of mountains stretching far across the plains. They would have to get over them to reach the other side. If only they could find a way to circumvent it – maybe walk across the distance to get behind the mountains. But the luxury of such time was what they didn't have.

THE RIVER UTA

The lovers arrived at the foot of the mountains. Like mountaineers, they sized them up. Measuring about 20 meters above the ground, they stood like giant, impenetrable fortresses. Latisha thought she could go over it. However, she was more concerned about Ren.

"How about we go across it to the other side?" she asked.

He had his eyes on the mountaintop, probably wondering how he would get up there. "That would take a long time. It's stretched over a long distance."

"These are tall mountains. Can you deal with the fear of falling as you go atop?" Latisha beamed with concern.

Ren glanced up at the top again. And with a bit of courage in his voice, he answered: "Yes."

Latisha recoiled. She knew he didn't mean that. He was only trying to be brave and save them some time. "Far less than a mile away from these mountains is the River Uta. You know that, don't you?"

"I do."

"So I do not want you getting wounded. It will slow us down and…"

"Do not let that bother you, my dear. I will be fine."

That sounded pretty reassuring! Latisha nodded, although glancing at him with a bit of doubt in her. "All right."

Latisha led the way this time. Her fingers dug into a pocket on the wall.

She gained traction and pulled herself up. Before she took the next step, she stopped and looked down. Ren stood at the foot of the mountain, looking up like some kid waiting expectantly for his mother to pluck him some oranges. Latisha did not say a word. She simply stared at him, perhaps as a way of urging him on.

He moved one step to the right and put his hand in a pocket on the wall. With that, he pulled his weight off the ground, almost leveling up with Latisha. "Come on," he called.

The wall had a jagged surface and small holes at different points. These provided traction as the lovers scaled the wall with bare hands. Ren panted for breath, putting in every effort necessary to keep his feet and hands steady.

"Do not look down," Latisha advised.

But with the determination he had shown, it didn't seem like he would lose his balance if he looked down for a moment. Latisha herself may not be afraid of heights, but getting up a 20-foot mountain on bare hands had its toll on her.

Ren dug into a hole in the wall and pulled himself up, but he placed his foot in the wrong spot and slipped.

"REN!" Latisha yelled, eyes wide with terror.

"I'm fine. I'm fine," he assured.

Luckily, he had a firm grip on the hole. He latched his hand on another part of the wall to support his weight. Latisha watched as he managed to regain his balance. She could hear her heart hammering against her chest. Perhaps she should listen to Ren's rhythm. It was literally stomping inside of him like a soldier's boots on the ground.

His hands and feet were shaking even as he tried to steady them on the wall. He kept swallowing lumps of saliva to help with his throat, which felt like he hadn't had water to drink for months. With steady, calm breathing, his whole system gradually returned to normal.

"Please be careful," Latisha warned as they continued.

For a moment, it seemed like the mountains grew taller – it seemed like they would never get to the top. But they did eventually. Latisha had slowed down so Ren could go ahead of her. She wanted to catch him should he slip again and fall. And with that, Ren was the first to reach the top of the mountains – a feat he thought was impossible. Latisha soon joined him.

The mountaintop treated them to a breathtaking view of nature for their efforts. Trees stood in place of pillars in a royal castle. Their canopies formed a unifying umbrella across the space. Lush greenery carpeted different parts of the ground. And in the sky, birds flew about like butterflies in a field of roses and daffodils.

From this vantage position, they would have espied the River Uta. But they could only see trees and more trees in that area.

"Are you sure that is where the River Uta is?" Ren questioned, standing on his toes and trying to see beyond the trees covering his view.

"It's been years, Ren – you don't expect the surroundings to look the same. We have to go."

Ren's hands were firmer on the walls, his feet stronger. Coming down was easier than going up. The force of gravity made it lighter, too. And carefully, they reached the ground.

"Here we are!" Latisha grabbed Ren and pulled him closer, leaning her groin against his. "It almost feels like you're no longer afraid of my heights, my king. Look how tall it is."

With a smile on his face, he looked up. Pride lit up his countenance and raised his shoulders. With that same smile, he looked back at Latisha. "I could have done it without you."

"Yes, you could have. I saw the determination in your eyes. I am proud of you, my king."

Ren felt like royalty indeed—from his smiles to the sudden feeling like he had the power to command anything, and it would come to pass. Latisha drew closer and kissed him softly on the lips. Her dimples sank graciously between her jaws, and smiles stretched the corners of her lips upon withdrawing.

Ren had his eyes closed when she kissed him. He had seen the fireworks exploding and felt butterflies in his stomach. Now that he had opened them, it felt like he had been given a new life. Nothing had felt as good as this kiss of commendation in a long time.

"This is our last lifetime together in these bodies," Ren spoke – his voice sounded like he was singing a lullaby. It had Latisha dissolving in his arms as they wrapped around her waist. "We have to get the sword and break the curse and then live happily till our final days."

Latisha looked deep into his eyes. "We shall bring forth children and raise them together. How beautiful it will be."

"As beautiful as you are, my queen." He rubbed down on her hair.

She smiled and rested her head on his chest. He continued to rub down on her hair. But the clock was ticking nonstop. The full moon hung somewhere in the night sky, getting ready to present itself on the third day.

With legs made of stone, the lovers continued on their way to the river. It was about 300 meters away from the mountains, and a straight path led to it. For them, traveling this distance on foot felt like going up and down the mountains 14 times without a break. To return to Palm Field, they would need a horse, Latisha thought. But she wasn't sure how they would get one.

The sun was only a few steps away into the horizon. Twilight was at the corners. The search for the sword could definitely not be at this time. As the better swimmer, Latisha thought she would begin in the morning.

"There should be a smell of mist as we approach the river. But the air is rather warm and dry," Ren observed.

"It is not always like that, I think."

"Believe me, my love, it is. The air is bereft of that familiar scent of the waters."

Latisha looked at him with a blend of uncertainty and curiosity in her eyes. "Are you insinuating that the River Uta has dried up?"

"It could be possible."

Yet she sighed, having realized how insanely impossible that was. It was hard to imagine that a river covering tens of meters would dry out. But in a few minutes, she would realize Ren was right after all.

As they got closer, more trees came into their field of view. They were stretching farther than a kilometer. At this point, Latisha had expected to perceive the scent of water or feel the lower temperature inherent around a large water body. But it was dry and warm, just like Ren had said. Now, the fear of the river drying up was starting to dawn on her.

"The river should be somewhere behind the woods," she told Ren as they stood at the edge of the forest.

It was what she had chosen to believe, yet the fear of uncertainty clutched at her heart.

"I hope so," Ren responded. It was pointless trying to convince her, he thought. It was better she saw it with her own eyes.

They crossed the edge of the forest, trudging across the floor carpeted by shrubs and dried leaves. The sun had given way. Overhead was a coating of grey. But with the canopy over the forest, most parts of it had already embraced darkness. Crickets and other insects gave a ceremonious melody. Even the bats joined the choir.

Dried sticks crackled underfoot as Latisha thumped deeper into the forest. She did not slow down. But Ren, who did his best to keep up, knew why she was like that. She was desperate to confirm that the River Uta still existed.

But after following the map in her head and arriving at the point she thought the river should be, reality began to set in.

"This is supposed to be the riverbank, and then the river itself spread out far," she cited, pointing

Ren looked around. The grey sky could still offer a level of visibility on the ground. Nothing stood as evidence that a river had been there. The surroundings were overgrown by trees and smaller plants. Maybe if he dug through the carpet, he would find white sand. Had he not known about the River Uta and its location, he would have sworn it never existed.

"I told you the river dried out."

Her face was as murky as the ruffled depth of a river. "But how?" It wasn't a small river. It covered this area," she lamented, voice heavy with anxiety.

"Anything is possible over the course of a hundred-plus years, my love."

She looked at the area once again. There was not even an illusion of a river anywhere. Her breathing quivered, as well as her voice: "What do we do now? How do we find the sword?"

Ren went closer and slid his hand across her neck, looking into her eyes laden with anxiety. "The River Uta used to be here. Although it is dried up, objects at the bottom could be lying around somewhere. All we have to do is look."

"It's a long time – what if we do not find it? What if someone else had taken it?"

"There is only one way to find out. But we cannot search the forest now. It is too late. We will make a fire and prepare our bedding for the night. We get some rest and begin in the morning."

His words defeated Latisha's fears and submerged her anxiety. She gazed at him, taking in some fresh air to calm the tension in her nerves.

Ren shared her anxiety, too. He just knew a better way to conceal it. Seeing how overgrown the forest was, it appeared they were doomed. It had been like this for many years – someone could have found the sword. He may not remember how it looked, but he guessed it would be some fancy blade.

Nevertheless, if they didn't find the sword, they would get over it, go home, and live their happiest moments. Perhaps they would be lucky during this time to find a solution. These were, however, thoughts Ren wouldn't share with Latisha just yet. The thought of their souls being condemned for all eternity was tormenting enough.

A DOOR IN THE FOREST

The wind found the forest. But it was not the kind that aroused suspicions of rain or something sinister. It was the kind that caressed the skin, the kind that made the night peaceful. Who could tell, however, that its movements would leave a delicate effect on the forest?

It was uncanny that one would sleep in a forest as though they were in their bedroom. Not even the mosquitoes were present. Ren and Latisha enjoyed one of the best nights in a long time. She had laid her head on his chest after they had kissed. And in his protection, they had passed the night at the foot of a sycamore tree.

The melodies of the Robins ushered in a new day. By the time they woke up, daylight had reached the forest floor.

"Good morning, my love." He slid his hand across her neck as they sat sideways, facing each other - reassuring smiles etched up on their faces.

"Good morning, my king," she replied, leaning her cheeks against his warm hand.

"I believe you slept well."

She nodded. "You slept well, too, right?"

"I have not slept this good in a long time. I guess nature is on our side to give us the strength we need for the search. We... is there a problem?

He had noticed the shock on her face as she looked behind him.

"Something is not right." She shuffled up on her feet, looking around the forest.

Ren got on his feet, too. "How do you mean?"

"The trees: they seem to have moved."

"What?" Ren's face crumpled like a piece of paper.

Latisha ran to the redwood nearby. "I saw this particular tree at the edge of the forest. I remember this scar right here," she pointed at a patch the size of a trash can lid on the bark of the tree. "And this one too." She dashed to another tree some feet away. "I saw it too while we were coming in. This cut…" she pointed at a cut 7 inches deep.

Ren surveyed the forest. But even with her proof, the trees stood innocent of her accusations. Not one of them appeared to have moved at all. The birds did not stop singing overhead, and the day did not stop dawning even brighter.

"Oh please, my love, do not look at me like that. I am certain of what I am saying."

Ren quickly looked away, not sure what to say. At this point, it was impossible to convince her that she was wrong. It was either he admitted she was right, or he would find a way to convince her otherwise.

He crouched down and began to brush the leaves off the ground in front of him.

"What are you doing?" she inquired.

"Looking for more evidence."

The word 'more' calmed Latisha a bit. It meant he believed her. She set her eyes on the ground, not entirely sure what he was looking for.

With his fingers, he dug into the ground and packed a handful of sand. Some grains filtered off like dust as he raised his hand.

"That's white sand from the river!" she exclaimed, moving closer to get a proper look.

"Yes. It means the River Uta was here."

"Exactly! But what I do not understand is how the trees moved."

"River Uta is believed to possess some magical powers. I believe it was the reason my mother came here to appeal to the goddess. It should not be surprising that trees growing in their original space move around."

Latisha nodded. "You are right."

"We have to look for the sword at once…"

It was not to dash her ego or make her look stupid, Ren believed now. He believed that as they slept, some strange force must have acted on the trees. It could, however, be of great benefit to them.

They kicked off the search. Latisha quickly grabbed a long piece of wood and began to scratch the surface around her and beyond. They looked under fallen branches and around the foot of every tree they reached.

But with the forest stretching more than a kilometer, it was impossible to search every part of it. They would have suffered the same fate if the river hadn't dried up. Plus, they did not consider the danger of coming face to face with poisonous snakes and scorpions.

Overhead, the sun had begun its journey from the east. Its rays broke through the canopy, revealing a thin cloud of dew in its path. Leaves rustled, and pieces of wood cracked as the search went on. Monkeys in the forest weren't comfortable with these uninvited noisemakers, and they aired their displeasure. They howled, chattered, and leaped from one tree to another.

"The monkeys are not happy that we are in their home," Ren observed, giggling.

"Definitely not! They would have sent us packing if they had their way."

"They are doing it the best way they can…"

As Ren returned to the search, Latisha looked down the forest. Its vastness was overwhelming. She thought it was impossible to search the whole of it in just one day. The reality of eternal condemnation of their souls was beginning to dawn on her, but she wouldn't give up. Ren already knew they were doomed, but not giving up drove them on. They believed a miracle could happen even in the final minutes.

So far, they had not come in contact with any dangerous snake. Raising some dead wood, they had only seen one or two scorpions and some centipedes. But the sighting of these animals was nothing compared to how heavy their waists felt. They had been searching for more than 2 hours, and their waists were starting to feel like they had a steel rod grafted between their upper and lower trunk. Latisha would growl lightly whenever she tried to stand straight. However, their misery was far from over.

"I think we should spread out," Ren suggested. "We will cover more grounds if we do."

With a wince up her features, Latisha stood straight, breathing through her mouth. "Okay."

"You are tired. Why don't we get some rest?"

"We do not have much time. The full moon is just around the corner."

After she had said these, she walked off to another part of the forest, about 10ft from her previous position. A feeling of guilt sprang up in Ren. According to Priestess Dara, he put them through this suffering. Maybe he should not have taken the sword. And even after he did and threw it into the water, his mother's blood initiated the course. Now Latisha shared it.

But even as his heart bled upon seeing her struggles, he tried to lighten his countenance. A sad moment would weaken their determination and cause them to surrender sooner rather than later.

While Latisha grubbed up dead leaves and splinters of wood in her new site, she noticed something: the log of wood she had turned upside down as she searched had turned to its original position, and the area around it looked like she hadn't been there.

It turned out that all the while they searched, they had not noticed that the grounds were reshuffling. The areas they had searched had been covered up, making the lovers come back to them again and again. It had been all about the search for Latisha—she would have noticed earlier.

She stood, gazing at the wood, with a crease between her brows. She turned it back and forth and looked carefully around it. She did not want to sound stupid while telling Ren about it. She had been here before. She had cleared this area before. The space between her brows drew even closer.

She looked up at Ren. It seemed like he hadn't covered a wide area. But she knew it was the same force at work. The area they had both worked on before they separated seemed the same, too - untouched.

She walked back to Ren. He saw her coming and straightened up, groaning, with his hand on his waist. "You want to get some rest?" he questioned.

"Look at the areas we have searched and tell me what you see." She came and stood in front of him.

Ren did as she instructed. But it was merely a glance. He soon turned to her. "I do not notice anything if that is what you mean."

"Look again."

He sighed. He looked again, not because he thought he would notice anything this time, but simply to please her.

Once again, he looked back at her and said, "I really do not know what you want me to see."

Her shoulders dropped at how he had failed to notice the details even when they were clear enough. "Do you not notice that the areas we have searched are closing up like we were never there?"

"What?" his brows snapped as he took another look. This time, he noticed it. His eyes flitted from one end to another – colors draining out of his face in surprise. "I know what this is…"

He ran to where they had started. The surroundings looked just like they had before they began the search.

Latisha met up with him. "You know what this is?"

"It is the Force of Reversal."

"Force of Reversal? What is that?"

"It is a powerful magic that reverses everything you do. It is usually cast on a sacred place to keep it from being transformed by human activities."

"But our actions would not cause any significant change in how the forest looks, right?"

"I don't know…" Ren's voice trailed off to nothing.

Latisha looked around once more. She was getting sated with so many conditions she had to tolerate. But it was clear to her she didn't have a choice. "You have any idea how we can break the spell?"

"One of us has to cut ourselves and let the blood drop on the ground. I am not certain if that will break the spell, but I think it is a chance we have to take."

"If you were not sure, why then did you say we should it?"

"Because someone told me about it, but he did not affirm if it worked or not."

Latisha weighed their options. The curse took effect because of the same blood ritual, and now they wanted to do it again. What if it turned out negative? What if it worsened their problem? Apparently, that was the only option at the table.

She shook her head. "And why does it have to be one of us?"

Ren was already looking for a sharp object for the job. "I don't know."

Rainclouds gathered on Latisha's face, proof that she was not comfortable with this plan. But Ren seemed to be quite confident about it. He eventually found a broken piece of metal and came and stood in front of her.

"Are you sure you want to do this?" her voice quivered.

"No, I'm not. But that's the only way."

They stared at each other, disbelief weighing on their minds. It felt like they were about to renew the curse, about to get it all wrong again.

Latisha crouched down and cleared the ground below Ren's hands, exposing the white sands of the River Uta of old.

She stepped back and watched. Ren held the rusty metal over his wrist, clenching his fist and breathing hard. The hand holding the metal jiggled with nervousness. But then he shrugged and flung his head sideways aggressively. It crackled like fireworks.

He placed the metal on his wrist. And with the speed of a guillotine, he swiped it against his skin. He yelped as the pain ripped through his nerves. Latisha crinkled her face, sharing in the pain.

Ren squatted and held his wrist over the spot she had cleared. It was more of a scratch than a cut, yet a glob of blood pooled at the surface. In a moment, a drop landed on the ground, and then another, and another.

Ren got on his feet and pressed hard on the spot with his thumb, having thrown away the blade. But Latisha ripped out a part of her shirt and moved closer. She tied the wound with the piece of cloth.

"That is it, right?" she asked, raising her eyes at him.

"Yes. And something should be happening by now."

A sigh escaped Latisha. "We should be patient. Come…"

She held his hand and led them to a nearby tree. They sat at the foot of the tree, leaning on it. As much as they feared the worst, they had high hopes that something good would happen.

Ren looked skywards. Only due to the forest's canopy did the rays of the sun not dazzle his eyes. It had reached the center of the sky and was now on its course westward.

"What do we do if it doesn't work, and how do we even know if it works?" Latisha inquired, adjusting her bottom on the ground.

Ren ruffled his black curly hair, combing off bits of plant shed. "Then we have to keep looking."

"We…" The rest of the words faded off.

Latisha wanted to object to that. But she quickly realized it was their only option. It would be unwise to completely abandon the search.

"What is it?" Ren looked at her, searching for the answer to his own question on her face.

"Never mind!" trepidation hung in her vocals.

With that blurry look on her face, Ren could tell what she wanted to say. But perhaps it was better left unspoken.

"If we find the sword before nightfall, then we will go on our way to Palm Field. We might get there before sunset. Much faster it will be if we can find a horse."

"I think we should be more concerned about finding the sword first."

That sounded more antagonistic than a mere opinion. It explained the abundance of what was going on in her mind. Ren felt it in her words. Perhaps it was best he kept quiet for a moment and allowed her emotion to spend itself.

It hadn't occurred to them the gentle breeze that had traveled through the forest as they talked. Their bodies had responded with goosebumps.

Ren had been doodling matchstick figures of them on the ground. And checking if Latisha had lightened up, he looked up at her. It was not her face he saw, but a door.

A brown door stood about 15 feet away. It was plain – no special carvings or markings, no frame or architrave – just a 200-cm door of sleek mahogany finish, standing almost in the middle of the forest with no kind of support. It had a golden handle glinting in the sun like a shard of glass.

"My love," Ren called, leaves rustling as he clambered up on his feet. His eyes set fixedly at the door as though it would disappear if he looked away for a moment.

Latisha followed the direction of his eyes. Hers widened upon seeing the door standing between two giant redwoods. She quickly got on her feet.

Ren held her hand as they padded closer to the door.

"I guess the spirits heard our supplication," Ren broke the silence that existed between them.

Latisha was dumbstruck. A barrage of thoughts was coming in and going out of her head: was this door a trap or some passageway to the sword?

They arrived at the door, staring at it and admiring how smooth and massive it looked. Ren checked out the sides. Each of the trees was 4 feet away from the door, and clearly, they provided no support for it. His eyes reached the ground, and again, he discovered it wasn't rooted to it.

The door appeared to have a strange, attractive glow that kept one enthralled. Latisha had fallen for this glow, and it took Ren's calls to snap her out of it.

"Are you okay?"

"Yes… I'm fine."

Ren observed her briefly and then turned to the door. "I guess we have to go through the door."

"Yes."

"I'll go first…"

"No, we'll go in together."

Fingers interlocked, they abandoned the demands of caution and stepped forward. Ren reached out for the door's handle. But then he stopped halfway, clenched his fist, released it, and pushed further.

His hand shook with fervor as he took hold of the handle. It felt cold under his touch, and his fingers curled tight as he turned it.

It was uncertain what lay behind this door, and there was no guarantee they would find the sword. Hope had led them on.

THE MAZE

When Ren opened the door, he found nothing behind it. It had led to nowhere as he and Latisha had expected. But as soon as they walked through, the door faded away like a lonely wisp of smoke.

And now, they stood at the entrance to a maze of vines. The walls towered more than 10ft above the ground, with the intricacy of a fish net. A narrow path led to either side – so narrow the lovers would have to walk one before the other if they must go through the same path.

"You take this way while I take that way," Latisha suggested.

Ren neither nodded nor said a word. He was not comfortable with that plan. It was dangerous going through a path they did not know where it would lead – worst of all, a maze. However, it didn't seem like he had much of a choice.

He went toward the left, Latisha toward the right.

"Careful," he whispered.

Latisha looked back. "You too."

Almost at the same time, they both disappeared behind their paths. It was the same pattern, although that of Latisha's seemed to be more convoluted. She navigated the paths, sparing some time to admire the lush green and white vines.

But as the maze stretched further, she broke off with a scuttle. The faster she went, the quicker she would get to the end. Ren thought the same, too. The maze obliged them, twisting and turning in different directions – from one path to another. At some point, Ren was tempted to call out to Latisha just to be sure she was okay.

Eventually, the maze narrowed into a path that led them back together. Ren came from the left, Latisha from the right. Their fingers interlocked again as they turned to the doorway that stood at the center.

Behind the doorway was a white cloud as thick as that in the sky – so thick it offered not the slightest visibility to whatever was behind it. The lovers looked at each other. Words weren't necessary – their eyes communicated their thoughts. It would be foolish of them to go back, having come this far.

Holding hands, they crossed the doorway into the cloud.

It felt like the initial temperature had dropped one degree. The clouds appeared to disperse steadily at the center as they took steps farther away from the doorway. In a short time, a space half the size of an average bedroom appeared at the center.

The clouds spread a little wider, revealing a Zweihander sword suspended in mid-air. Its silver blade reflected the white clouds. Its handle appeared black from a distance, with a red patch somewhere in the middle.

Latisha's mouth gaped as she stared fixedly at it. "That's the sword," she commented.

The sound of her voice echoing through the clouds took her attention away from the sword for a moment. She looked around. But all there was were white clouds.

"Hello!" Ren called – his voice echoed even louder.

"You are welcome," a voice replied.

And as they looked around to decipher from which direction it had come, a man emerged from the clouds. He was about the length of a spade, putting on a brown coat that reached his ankles. He had a full beard bordered by what looked like a handlebar mustache. With his hands locked behind him, he marched to where the sword was and stood by it, staring back at the two pairs of awestruck eyes.

"I am Melkis, the sword keeper. I have been waiting for you," he added.

Ren rubbed his right fingers together like he was about to snap them. "We-we are here for the sword."

"I know. And here it is." He gestured.

Once again, their eyes fell on the blade hanging in mid-air. From one end to another, it measured about 150cm, gleaming with luxuriance and majesty.

"Can- can we take it?" Ren asked, glancing up at Melkis.

"It has been waiting for you through generations. But you must understand that only the female human can wield it."

The lovers looked at each other and then back at Melkis. "Why?" Latisha inquired.

"The male human must by no circumstance touch the sword. Not only will it lose its powers, but will bring destruction to the living. With all pleasure, please go ahead and take the sword."

The lovers shared a glance once again. Latisha felt the reluctance in her muscles, yet the eagerness to go for that object they had been through it all for.

Her feet broke off the ground as she plodded forward. Her heart thudded with an irregular rhythm. Suspense hung in the air as Ren and Melkis watched. To Ren, it was as though a bomb would go off immediately after she touched the sword.

She got to the sword and stared at it for a while – and then she looked at Melkis. He nodded lightly. It was with one last bit of strength that she wrenched her hand from her side against the force holding it back. Her fingers trembled lightly – but eventually, she took hold of the handle.

She had expected a kind of power surge immediately after her hand met the sword. But even as she plucked it off the air, she felt nothing. She raised it, admiring the sleekness of a Zweihander. Blood was starting to return to Ren's face as he gazed with admiration, too. Melkis simply looked up at the sword. He seemed dissatisfied, knowing that the initiation was not complete yet.

Just as Latisha turned toward Ren, her hands vibrated vigorously. It was quickly transmitted to other parts of her body, making her knees buckle. She staggered back and forth.

"What is going on?" Ren questioned, charging forward.

But Melkis raised his hand, halting his movement. "To become the new keeper till it is returned to its rightful place, she must become one with the sword."

Ren was left with no choice but to watch as Latisha gyrated with the sword in her hand. Her knees were giving away as she lolloped like a drunkard. But as if bearing the egg of a dragon, she kept her feet on the ground, clutching onto the sword.

In an instant, the force disappeared. Latisha regained her balance. With the sword in her hand and her feet still on the ground, it was a victory.

She was pumping air into her lungs. Helpful was how light the sword was in her grasp.

"Well done!" Melkis commended – satisfaction gleamed on his face this time. "Until the sword is returned to its rightful place at the Mighty Rocks, you shall guard it with your life. Not even the 7 elders of Apokata are allowed to wield it."

Latisha nodded. Her eyes drooped with exhaustion as she trudged back to meet Ren.

He draped his hand across her shoulders as they headed for the doorway.

"Remember, no human male must wield the sword," Melkis warned one last time.

They had turned upon hearing his voice. Now, the clouds wrapped them in a teleporting embrace.

The next moment, they found themselves in the middle of the forest. Latisha still had the sword in her hand.

"He brought us back to the forest," Ren commented as his eyes got acquainted with the surroundings.

At this time, the sun had retired and the sky had turned grey.

Latisha held the sword up as efficiently as a gladiator. "We have a long way ahead of us. Let's go."

"Which way are we headed?" he asked as though the sword had a map on it.

"East," she answered – a closer route to Palm Field.

As they turned in the direction, they spotted two men coming their way. Their swords dangled from their horses as they rode closer. They had thick beards and looked slightly brawny behind their jackets.

Ren knew trouble was cooking. The men might develop an interest in the sword. A fight would break out, and then one of them might end up getting hold of it. It was a risk they couldn't afford – not this time.

"Those men might try to attack us. If they do, I want you to run through the east as fast as you can. I will try to stall them as long as I can. If I don't meet up with you, don't stop until you get to Palm Field. I will find you there. Understand?"

"Yes," Latisha grudgingly answered after a few seconds.

She wouldn't abandon Ren to face the men alone if she wasn't with the sword.

Ren's face assumed a frown to ward off any evil intent. But that had no effect on the men.

One of them alighted from the horse, and with a smirk, Latisha wished she could slap off his face. Of course, she knew what that meant.

"Only a coward would allow his woman to wield the sword," the man's voice came over the creaks and buzzes of insects, leaving his horse's reins and walking closer.

"He is weak and obviously needs his woman to protect him," the other man added.

One of the horses snorted. It could have been asking for justice for Ren, but the man interpreted it differently.

"See, even the horse agrees."

But the lovers completely ignored them and continued on their way. One of the men went back and drew his sword. Latisha held tight to hers, waiting for Ren's signal to take off.

"You don't walk away when I'm talking to you." He leveled his sword at the lovers, keeping them in a spot

"Aren't you going to say something? Are you scared?" his friend stepped closer. It was more of a mockery than a question. But as Ren did not reply, he turned his attention to Latisha. "That's some nice blade you got there, lady."

And that was the man overstepping his boundaries! Ren and Latisha exchanged glances. She got the message.

Like a bull gathering some momentum for a clash of horns, she drew backward, observing the men's body language all the while.

"What are you doing?" one of them asked – laughter etched upon his face.

But Latisha had already pulled 5 feet backward, and off she sprinted. Now, it dawned on him what she was doing.

"STOP RIGHT THERE!"

The man stomped forward, but Ren stood in his way. "Let her go, man."

"And who's going to stop us?" he leveled his sword at Ren.

"I will."

The men sized him briefly and then broke off with laughter. Ren was just as brawny as they were. His hard, slightly protruded cheeks affirmed his masculinity. It was hard for one not to feel the tension when those pair of blue eyes glared down at them. But even with these, the men didn't think he was a match for them, probably because he was outnumbered, two to one. And with their horses, they were confident they would catch up with Latisha and so did not bother going after her immediately.

The wrinkles faded, and the man's face darkened like the sky overhead. "Stand in my way again, and I shall cut you through."

His friend had already got on his horse. But Ren broke his silence, keeping him from riding off.

"Ignorance looks good on you two. But even more stupid are you to think you would get to her."

The one on the horse got down. His friend charged forward and swung his sword at Ren. But he leaped backward.

"You can do better than that," he urged him.

The other man joined in the fight. "After we kill you, we will find your lady, lie with her as many times as we want, kill her, and take the sword."

"I'd like to see you try," Ren answered.

Whatever gave him this confidence must have been reassuring. The men looked skilled with the sword. Standing up to them meant he was on a death wish.

One of them flung his sword to slice off his head. But he ducked. At the same time, the other man tried to drive the sword through his belly. Ren dived out of the way.

"COME ON!" he blared.

That aroused the men who felt their ego was being squashed underfoot like a cockroach. With rage in their hands, they swung their swords at Ren. But expertly, he defended himself. One man rolled across the ground, going for his leg, but he leaped up. And as the other man tried to slice his belly, he dived behind them.

He landed on the ground. And as he got on his feet, he parked handfuls of sand. The men wasted no time charging forward. But a stream of sand spattered their faces. One of them yelled. And as they both stood back, rubbing their eyes, Ren ran to the horses. He quickly mounted on, charged it up, and rode off.

And that had been his plan all along. He never intended to fight the men. He wanted to lure them as far away from their horses as possible and run back for one. His plan worked. And while they rubbed on their eyes and yelled for him to stop, having heard their horse's shoes thumping the ground, he rode toward the east.

PALM FIELD

Ren had caught up with his lover. It had been a struggle running with the sword. It was starting to gain weight under her grip. In fact, he had found her leaning back against a tree, swallowing mouthfuls of air. He had helped her up the horse, making sure not to touch the sword.

They had ridden all night, resting only for a short time. Finally, they arrived at Palm Field in the early hours of dawn.

They were by the edge of the field, observing. Only a few people were outside at this time, most of whom were guards. Life had yet to begin.

"I keep wondering how we are going to convince them to help us," Latisha spoke. "They might have us locked up in their cellars or even kill us on sight."

"But why will the gods bestow upon their elders the cleansing powers? They aren't clean."

Latisha let out a sigh. "We cannot always understand the ways of the spirits. Let's go – we're running out of time."

Ren tugged on the reins and kicked the horse lightly. It rode them on toward the heart of Palm Field. It was perhaps the final hurdle remaining to cross.

The guards leveled their weapons at them as they got closer. One of them accosted the lovers, with his sword ready to dismember them.

"You must have deemed your lives worthless coming back here again."

"We come in peace. Please let us through," intoned Ren as the horse pulled over. About 10 men surrounded them, all directing their weapons at them.

The guard shifted glances between Latisha and the sword in her hand – then he looked up at Ren. "What do you want?"

"We want to have a word with the queen."

The guard glanced at the sword again. He seemed to realize it was no ordinary sword. He stood aside. A look of relief washed over the lovers' faces. They had just passed their first encounter.

They were led through to the queen's quarters. Ren alighted and helped Latisha down. She held the sword up like a treasure, not letting it touch the ground. The guard gestured at the door and led the way.

It was an empty courtroom, with only the queen's throne at the far end. Sculptures of humans and bulls were carved off the walls – behind the throne was that of a lion, more like a gargoyle.

Ren and Latisha stood before the throne, surrounded by four armed guards. It appeared someone had gone behind to inform the queen of their presence, for in a short while, she emerged through a door on the right side of her throne.

Her slender frame masked the body Latisha thought would be in its early 40s. Even so, she thought she looked adorable in her long black dress. Her blond hair flowed down her back in waves – its fullness added more weight upon which her golden crown balanced. Ren gazed at her with the same inquisitiveness as Latisha. It appeared he did not set his eyes on her the last time he was here.

"Greetings, my queen," the lovers greeted, bowing lightly.

Latisha observed the queen's eyes move from Ren to her and then to the sword in her hand.

"Who are you, and what are you doing in my kingdom?"

Ren spoke first, introducing himself and Latisha. "We are from Utria and have come to seek your help."

"My help?" The queen kept a focused gaze at them, all the while standing by her throne.

"The Curse of Reincarnation was placed on us generations ago. We had no idea about it until our 4th lifetime. Ever since then, we have been looking for a way to lift the curse. It is our 7th lifetime, and now we have finally found a way. We were told by a priestess of the old religion that only the 7 elders of Apokata can lift the curse, using this sword (gesturing). And that is why we have come."

The queen looked briefly at the sword again. Her chest dropped with a breath. "Who is this priestess you speak of?"

"Priestess Dara of the Island of Reprieve."

While Ren answered her question, a guard moved in and whispered something to the queen's ear. Now, she has settled her attention on Ren.

"I hear you have been here before."

"Yes, Your Majesty."

"And you were supposed to be my mate."

Ren did not respond. Jealousy and possessiveness were starting to light up in Latisha's eyes.

"Well," the queen continued, "I shall grant your request on one condition: you shall lie with me in my chambers."

Latisha's fingers curled tighter on the sword. Her cheeks went scarlet as she glared at the queen. She thought it disrespectful that she would demand for that even after Ren told her she was his woman.

"My apologies, Your Majesty, but is there no other way?" Ren inquired. Having seen the guard whisper something to her ear, he knew their chances of getting help became slimmer.

"There is no other way."

Ren could see all their efforts crumbling right before his eyes. But for the sanctity of his love for Latisha… "Please forgive me, Your Majesty, but I'm afraid I have to decline your request. I…"

"Then I cannot help you. And for all the loss you inflicted on my people, I ask that you leave my kingdom immediately."

A mist of sweat spread across Ren's face. "Your majesty, I ask that you please reconsider your decision."

"Leave my kingdom and never come back. The consequences will be severe if you ever do." Her wrinkles had taken a twist, and her cheeks flushed.

There was nothing they could do at this point. Her decision appeared to be set in stone. She was not willing to consider anything else. Ren knew they had hit rock bottom, and it was time to leave.

"Ever since we discovered we were plagued with the Curse of Reincarnation, we have been looking for a way to lift it. Through 4 generations, we stuck together. Our love was pure and undying. We remained faithful to each other while looking for a way to be free. We went through it all – the efforts, the failures, the emotional torments, and the hopelessness. For all that you believe in, Your Majesty, do you think it is fair for us to die with a curse that will condemn our souls for all eternity?"

Latisha had chosen her words carefully. Her heart drummed as she spoke, not because she hoped the queen would reconsider her decision, but to subtly say she was the reason their souls would be condemned.

The queen gazed intently at her. She seemed surprised by her outburst, even though it was done with all modesty. Ren had looked briefly at Latisha as she spoke. Now he hoped her words would make the difference. And it did...

"What is your name?" the queen inquired.

"Latisha, Your Majesty."

"You seem to have a way with words, Latisha." She exhaled deeply. "Well... I respect the purity of love and what it stands for. And for that, I shall grant your request..."

CURSE LIFTED

With pearls floating in it, the White River was true to its name. Covering an expanse of space, it looked like it had been painted white. It was surrounded by palm trees, with heights measuring almost equal to those of redwoods.

The seven elders of Apokata stood at the shore of the river, putting on white hooded robes. The lovers could swear they had no idea what their faces looked like, for they were concealed in the thick hoods.

But their looks mattered not at this point. The elders had expressed that the ritual be done at sunset, and the full moon was on its way. The lovers wanted the ritual completed as quickly as possible.

"The ritual is of two parts."

"You must complete one before the other for the curse to be lifted."

"For they are like two sides of a coin."

"You must face your worst fears."

"And emerge victorious."

"Eternity of torment and condemnation awaits if you fail."

"Are you ready?"

The elders had spoken one after the other, with their heads bent.

The lovers looked at each other briefly, being reminded of their worst fears. But at this point, they were willing to go through a burning furnace to free themselves of the curse.

"Yes, we are," they both answered.

The last two elders who spoke pointed their fingers at them. Instantly, they dropped from their ground, completely removed from their environment. The sword lay beside Latisha.

But it was not with her when she found herself in the middle of a river, struggling to keep her head above the water. She bucked and kicked as she bobbed up and down like a ping-pong ball. Her hands waved frantically in the air.

There was no one else in the river covering several kilometers. She called for help. But the water in her throat muffled the sound of her voice.

She was losing strength with every struggle. Her head no longer came fully out of the water. Her hands grew weaker, too.

After a while, she got lost in the water, and not a part of her made it afloat. Deep in the water, she could feel life draining out of her.

But all of a sudden, she opened her eyes and burst out of the water. Air rushed through her mouth, down her lungs. And as it filtered into her muscles, she found strength again.

With the expertise of a diver, she swam toward the shore, arms waving like a penguin's flippers. The distance was about a kilometer or more, but she was determined to make it.

Meanwhile, Ren was on his way down from the peak of a mountain taller than a Sequoia tree. It had taken him a great deal of mental strength not to have plunged himself down the mountain. Gravity kept pulling him. The voices in his head kept urging him, convincing him that it was impossible to reach the ground safely. But he had ignored the forces.

And not letting tension and anxiety overwhelm his muscles, he took one step at a time down the mountain. He had it rough along the way. His legs shook with tremors. His blood pressure rose to a certain level, flattened, and then spiked. He dared not look at the ground below. Consistently he went, breathing hard and trying to stay sane.

Eventually, they both conquered.

Although their faces were obscure, the elders must have been impressed when the lovers opened their eyes. They both looked exhausted.

Ren took Latisha's hand, glad that they both made it through.

The ritual had taken almost an hour. The sun was fast disappearing into the horizon, and the elders must hurry.

And now, Latisha and Ren stood in the river in their underwear, the water reaching their waists. They faced each other, holding hands.

"No matter what happens, do not let go of your hands till the end of the ritual," the elders had warned.

Following their instructions, Latisha had buried the sword in the sands between them, with a quarter of its blade and handle jutting out of the water.

The elders had been mumbling a silent prayer and holding hands all the while. Now, they raised their hands toward the heavens and beckoned on the seven lords. Each one of them stood as a solicitor for seven lifetimes. And they all prayed in different languages, yet it was harmonious.

For several minutes, they continued to call on the seven lords, asking for mercy on behalf of the lovers. Their voices traveled across the river and beyond the palm trees. At first, it seemed like their prayers would not be answered, but the elders were listening.

The river began to glow—even brighter was the area around the sword. The river's whiteness reflected the lights, making it look like a giant glasshouse. Leaves and branches swayed in a sudden blast of wind. It got stronger as the elders prayed. The lovers held tight as the wind tugged at their hands, threatening to prize them apart.

A light appeared around the sword – so bright it would have blinded the lovers instantly had their eyes been open. Even so, it penetrated the lids that they had to shut them tighter. Gradually, the sword emerged from the water, glowing as bright as the sun. At this time, the river was at its brightest too. The voices of the elders resounded as one.

The sword came and hung itself between the lovers. Then, the light around it expanded slowly and covered the lovers in a ball as big as a tent. They glowed like angels making a special appearance. But it was not just the light. As it expanded, it carried with it a light stream of water, and the lovers were drenched in it.

Even as they were immersed in the lights, the wind did not stop pulling on their hands. It was as though it had all its force around them. Latisha was getting weak, but Ren held on. His hands wobbled. The elders were still holding hands, too, but there was no force around them.

The lights lasted for minutes, and the lovers struggled to keep their hands locked on. Gradually, the sword began its journey back into the water, carrying the lights with it. The wind was starting to lose its force. Ren might have thought he was gaining strength as he felt the relief around his wrists.

The sword submerged in the water, as did the lights, the wind, and the forces. The White River gradually regained its original color. The trees gained more control of the wind. Nonetheless, the elders didn't stop praying.

After a while, it all faded away. Latisha and Ren opened their eyes. It was blurry at first, but slowly, their eyes got acquainted with their surroundings. How beautiful it was to see each other's faces again! They knew the curse had been lifted. It was evident in their smiles. But like a patient waiting for the physician's report, they would have to get confirmation from the elders.

"You may come out of the water," one of them commanded.

Finally, they unlocked their hands, taking deep breaths. Latisha bent over to take the sword, but another elder advised otherwise:

"Leave the sword in the water for now."

She withdrew her hand. She took hold of Ren's instead as they sloshed out of the water.

They looked like they had gone through a rebirth. Their bodies shone in the orange sun. Latisha's hair was soaked with water, and strands of it matted on her forehead, neck, and shoulders. Their eyes twinkled with relief.

"The lords are merciful."

"You are free."

"Only the female human must return to the water and retrieve the sword."

"You two shall journey back to the Mighty Rocks."

"You will find a cluster of 7 at its very heart."

"Thrust the sword through and go your way."

"Do not look back."

The elders spoke.

The lovers' smiles were as bright as the lights they had just come from. A wave of relief overwhelmed their senses. And from its abundance came the words:

"Thank you."

The elders walked to the river and lined across its shore, their feet soaked in the water. The lovers weren't sure what they were doing as they were backing them, but it seemed like they were praying.

Shortly after, they all washed their hands in the water. After they had done that, they turned and walked away.

Latisha and Ren wrapped themselves in an affectionate embrace. It was over. Generations of struggles to set themselves free – dying and coming back to life and continuing on their quest – all that they endured. It was like they were carrying the world on their shoulders.

But now the weight had been lifted – the curse haunted them no more. If they were to return in the next life, they were certain this time that it wouldn't be in their original form. And perhaps they would meet each other and fall in love again. Until then, they would enjoy the remainder of their years in this lifetime, free from the curse.

Conclusion

In the shadows of destiny and through the storms of trials, Latisha and Ren's journey was a testament to the power of unwavering love and the indomitable human spirit. As the celestial event that once threatened to seal their fates fades into the cosmos, our heroes emerge, not unscathed but undeniably transformed.

Their path, riddled with sacrifices and haunted by spectres of past sins, led them to confront not just external malignancies but also the depths of their own souls. The curse, a malevolent chain that bound them across lifetimes, ultimately proved to be the crucible in which their true spirits were forged.

The illusion of freedom shattered, but from its shards rose a clearer, harsher truth—that some battles must be fought over and over, not for victory, but for the chance to fight again, together. And so, Latisha and Ren learn that true liberation isn't about breaking free from the curse but about embracing the bond that it forged between them, a bond not of shackles but of choice, love, and renewal.

As our story closes, they stand on the threshold of a new beginning, aware that peace is not the absence of conflict but the presence of love. For in each other, they have found their eternal bond, their light through lifetimes, and the courage to face whatever new challenges the cosmos might cast in their star-crossed journey.